his call

EMMA HART

Copyright © 2014 Emma Hart

All rights reserved.

ISBN-13: 978-1500164973

ISBN-10: 1500164976

Dedication

For everyone who loved Aaron and Dayton.

For all your excitement, swooning, begging, and panty-changing. Your love for these characters blows me away.

You made me want to be inside his head. It's a wonderfully dirty place to be.

This one is for you.

This CALL series novella consists of scenes from Aaron's POV. Find out what he was thinking during some of your favorite scenes from *LATE CALL* and *FINAL CALL*. Enjoy two exclusive scenes from when Aaron and Dayton were apart, and read about what happened with that little red outfit in a never-before-seen scene in this novella only.

I myself am made entirely of flaws, stitched together with good intentions.

Augusten Burroughs

The One Where They Meet Again

I step from the car and adjust my tie, my eyes falling on the Southfall Hotel in front of me. My reason for being here is merely to be a scapegoat, to take the pressure off of my father's retirement.

And the rest of the functions over the next few weeks, both here and abroad, are all for show. To let Naomi know that, unless she signs those divorce papers, she'll be walking away with a little less. It's a petty, childish game I'd rather pass over—much like our divorce. Petty.

I bat those thoughts from my mind for the evening and approach the reception desk. The young woman behind the counter smiles at me.

"Good evening, sir, and welcome to the Southfall Hotel. How

can I help you?"

"I have a private booth booked in the bar. Mr. Stone."

She smiles. "Ah, of course, Mr. Stone. And a…Ms. Lopez?"

"That's correct. Can you send her through when she arrives?"

"Of course. If you follow Neil here, he'll take you to your booth."

"Thank you"—I glance at her name badge—"Rachel."

She gives me another kind smile as I follow the young boy into the dimly lit bar. He stops in front of a curtained booth and slides it along the rail.

"Your booth, sir. Can I get you anything to drink?"

"Ah, no, thank you. I'll wait until my date arrives."

"Very well." He nods and turns, leaving me to enter the booth alone.

Yes. My date.

The date I required but didn't have. The date I'm being forced to pay for although the very thought is against everything I believe in. Paying for a woman's time seems derogatory and demeaning, no matter how willingly it's offered.

I lean back in the seat, exhaling deeply, and rest my hands on the table. Shit, I'd give anything to not have to do this charade. I'd do anything not to—

"Thank you."

I recognize her voice before she opens the curtain. I'd know it anywhere—that seductive tone that falls straight to my cock the way it did the first time I heard her speak. Every hair on the back of my neck stands to attention in anticipation of the woman I know I'm about to stare at.

But I fight to keep my eyes down. Fuck, I want to look at her. I want to see how much she's changed, see how different she is as a woman than the girl I fell in love with.

A sharp intake of breath follows the swish of the curtain shutting. Then I hear the sweetest fucking sound I've heard in a long time—my name from her lips.

"Aaron?"

I look up now, straight into the gorgeously dark eyes of the woman I never imagined I'd ever see again. My eyes comb over her. Her long, dark hair, curled slightly at the ends. Her wide, coffee-colored eyes shining with the shock I feel taking my own body hostage. Her glossy, pink lips that look as soft as they were.

She's the same but so different. She's older, curvier...and so much fucking sexier. A fact that makes my cock twitch inside my pants.

"Dayton?" I stand slowly, never taking my eyes from her.

"What..." She puts a hand to her chest, steadying herself. "*You're* my client?"

I wave toward the seat, unable to believe she's standing here. In front of me. Wondering why the fuck she is and where the hell Mia Lopez is. She sits slowly, her chest rising and falling quickly, and I gaze at her.

"You're my date? I hired a Mia Lopez?"

"Mia is my working name," she says quietly, glancing down. "Being an escort is a double life."

Dayton is an escort? A call girl? *My* Dayton?

"I can't believe this." I push a button and a waiter appears. "A bottle of Pinot Gris. Two glasses," I order without looking at him.

My eyes are locked on the woman in front of me. The woman whose body I know as well as my own yet whose mind is a complete enigma to me. I can't imagine any reason she'd do this, what could possibly possess to put herself in a situation to be taken advantage. Why she'd offer a body as wonderful as hers to an unlimited amount of men.

Fuck. My jaw clamps shut. That thought…

Silence lingers until the waiter reappears with the bottle of wine. I take it from him with a slight nod of acknowledgement and drag my eyes from Dayton long enough to pour two glasses of wine.

I reach into my inner jacket pocket, pausing before my fingers close around the envelope. Fuck. This is wrong. This is so fucking wrong. I loved this woman once. I shouldn't be paying her for her time.

Still, I pull it out and slide it across the table. Dayton drains her glass in one go, her actions belying her composed stature, and takes the envelope without blinking.

"Thank you."

"This was unexpected."

"Ya think?" She looks at me now, her eyebrows arching over her eyes. "I can't say I'm in the habit of having a previous personal relationship with my clients."

"I'd imagine not." I say my thought out loud, but it's not my most potent thought. That's why. Why she would do this. "Can I ask why?"

"Why what?"

"Why you do this?"

She bristles, clearly uncomfortable with my line of questioning. "That's a bit personal."

I lean forward on the table, my eyes steady on hers. "Dayton, I've seen every inch of your body. Don't fuck around and tell me it's too personal."

"You're my client." She sits up straighter, her jaw clenching slightly. "Our past is irrelevant here. You're paying me to do a job, and I'm going to do it. No personal details. Tell me what I need to know so I don't look like a complete idiot when I'm out there tonight."

My own jaw tightens at her indifference. I reach up and adjust my tie to stop myself from smacking my hand on the table and calling her on it. Instead, I take a deep, calming breath and take a sip from my glass.

"Dad has decided to step back from the company, and this is one of many events designed to introduce me to the people I'll be working with when I take over in just under two months."

"The modeling agency?"

"We branched into advertising and rebranded the summer after Paris. It went global three years ago, and now there are offices in Australia and Europe as well as here."

"Impressive. And you needed a date because?" She tilts her

head to one side.

I smirk. "Because if I turned up alone, the vultures would get me."

"The vultures?"

"The daughters of my mother's friends. They're single."

"And you're the perfect target. Nice to know I'm hired to be a buffer."

"I'm sure Mia Lopez is used to it." Bitterness coats my statement, but she doesn't seem to notice it. She simply raises her glass to her lips and lets some wine fall between them.

"Oh, she is," she replies with an easy confidence. "But we both know there's not a chance in hell I'll get away with being Mia tonight."

I consider this. She's correct—my parents will surely recognize her. If I did so easily, they will, too. We spent more than enough time together in Paris. I run my tongue across my bottom lip, debating my next move.

Her eyes flick to my mouth and she draws in a breath. I smirk. She can play the indifference card, but that moment alone has told me that she's still affected by me. Just as much as I am by her.

"Mr. Stone?" a voice asks from behind the curtain.

"Yes?" I reply without taking my eyes from hers. A slight flush rises in her cheeks when she realizes I've caught her staring.

"Your father is asking for you, sir."

"Tell him we'll be there momentarily."

"Of course."

My father. Dayton... Her identity.

I reach across the table and take my hand in her. "Day, you don't have to do this. You have a working name for a reason. I won't ask you to jeopardize that for me."

She snatches her hand as if my touch is burning her and stands. She smooths out her dress, taking a moment before her eyes meet mine again. "You hired me to do this job, and I'm going to do it. Besides, I can't have you being eaten alive by the vultures, can I?"

She wants to play that card... I smirk again. "Very true."

I stand and pull the curtain open, my eyes crawling over her body as she walks in front of me. Fuck. Now that the initial shock of seeing her again has passed, I can appreciate the sight before me. Appreciate the way her waist curves into shapely hips and long legs—legs I know are long enough to wrap around my waist.

Fuck.

I place my hand on her back, guiding her into the elevator. She jolts a little, like my touch is so unexpected, and I revel in the fact she feels as shaken as I do. I know her so well, and standing next to her right now is like we've never been apart.

But I won't let her do this if she doesn't want to. I won't force her into it. I respect her too much...but obviously not enough to have sent her home the moment she walked to the booth. Obviously not enough to not pay her.

The elevator doors open, and I close them again.

She looks at me with a frown. "What are you doing?"

"Dayton." I raise my hand to her face and brush some hair from her eyes.

She bats it away, her eyes flashing with memories of the past. "Standing in an elevator isn't going to change the fact I have a job to do, Aaron. Can we get on with this?"

I watch her for a long moment, scrutinizing every inch of her face, making sure she's not just putting on a show. Of course she is. I'm putting on a fucking show. I don't want to take her into some bullshit function. I want to take her back down to that bar, buy her dinner, and find out what the hell she's been doing for the last seven years. Aside from being paid to sleep with other guys, a fact that riles and awakens every protective instinct in my body.

An instinct that makes me want to do something about it.

I incline my head toward her, treating her with the same calm she is me. "Fine. But what do I tell my parents when they inevitably recognize the girl who stole me for the duration of our vacation seven years ago?"

She licks her lips and swallows. "You let me think of that."

I push the button to open the doors and lead her in the direction of the ballroom. I rest my hand on the ornately decorated door and look down at her. "Last chance," I murmur.

She sighs. "Shut up and open the damn door for me."

I laugh quietly, grateful for the spark in her voice. The genuine spark that breaks through her façade and makes me ache for Paris. Makes me ache for her, her voice, her touch, her body.

We walk into the room together, my hand creeping to her hip, and the second my parents notice us, I know.

I know there isn't a fucking chance I'm letting Dayton Black walk away from me a second time.

The One Where They Have A Second First Time

She looks fucking beautiful.

She's a vision in that turquoise lace, and I've barely been able to keep my eyes off of her. The way it hugs her body like a second skin has had my cock twitching inside my pants all night, and now I'm almost ready to drag her out of here and take her to our room.

Almost.

For a minute longer, I watch her. I watch the way she smiles, her face lighting up as she does, and the gentle way she pushes her wayward hair from her face. I watch the way she lifts her glass to her mouth and sips the wine inside. The way her throat bobs as she swallows, and my eyes settle on her chest as she laughs, making her perky tits jerk with the motion.

Shit... Fuck... I swallow the last of my drink as the woman she was talking to leaves and crosses the room. My eyes never leave Dayton. Nothing is stopping me from taking this woman upstairs and burying my cock inside her tonight.

I throb at the thought, blood rushing downward and hardening my dick. She turns away from me and brings her glass to her lips again.

"We're going," I whisper behind her, my lips brushing the nape of her neck.

"It's still early." Amusement threads through her tone—amusement I plan to fuck right out of her.

"Turn around."

Slowly, she does as I say and rests her hands on my chest. I lower my face to hers, keeping our eye contact, and she draws in a long breath.

"Now tell me, do I look like a give a fuck?"

Dark eyes flick over my face. "No."

I wrap an arm around her back, my hand settling on her waist, and whisper, "Then let's go."

Full of certainty, I lead her through the busy room. Everyone who glances our way is met with my hard stare. I'm not stopping. Not this time. Not ever. Not with Dayton.

I jab the button on the elevator impatiently.

"No goodbyes?" she mutters.

I flip her toward the elevator and lean against her. Her body is soft beneath mine, and I take advantage of the slight part of her lips by covering them with mine. "I'm going to be inside you within the hour and you're worried about saying goodbye?"

Her quick intake of breath is audible.

"Hmm?" I push my hips into her.

"No. Not worried."

Good, I think, wrapping a hand around her neck and taking her mouth prisoner with mine. I kiss her firmly and desperately, letting her know how much I need her. Fuck, does she even know? Can she even comprehend the way I need to feel her bare skin against mine?

I break the kiss and back into the suite, tugging her with me. I meet her eyes and show her the truth of my words in my gaze, because I mean every fucking bit of it.

"Leave it," I demand sharply. "All the client bullshit, all the money, and all the obligations. Leave it in the motherfucking elevator and tell me you want me. Tell me you want me to fuck you so hard the only thing you'll be able to scream by the end of the night is my name."

She says nothing, just stares at me, her cheeks flushing.

"Say it!" I pull her closer, harshly, demandingly.

"I want you!" Her voice is small but strong. "Fucking hell. I shouldn't but I do. I want you."

"How badly?"

"Don't push it."

I dig my fingers into her skin and lower my face. "How fucking badly?"

"So bad that if you don't kiss me right this fucking second I might hit you!"

My lips crash into hers with the ferocity I feel inside. I need this woman naked and I need my cock inside her. There will be nothing slow or loving about this. There's too much rawness for this to be anything but intense and hard. There's too much time passed. Too much desperation to feel completeness once more.

Her fingers find my jacket as I nibble on her bottom lip and she pushes it over my shoulders.

"Want me or need me?" I clarify.

"Shut up and take it off before I rip it off." There's a quiet moan in her voice, and a rush goes through me at the thought that she's as affected by me as I am by her.

"You forgot something." I unzip her dress, allowing my fingertips to ghost down her spine.

"What's that?"

"My name."

She pulls back and her eyes bore into mine. "I'm about to rip your shirt off, *Mr. Stone*. Are you okay with that?"

My cock throbs. "Not really."

"Tough shit." A smile plays on her lips as she does it anyway.

I push her against the wall and sweep my tongue through her mouth in one long, possessive stroke. So she understands that no other man will ever fucking touch her the way I am right now. The way I plan to. No other man will ever see her come.

She whimpers into my mouth, a sound that makes me kiss her harder. She drops her hands to my belt, and I step back.

"Hell no. Don't you remember what I said?"

I feel her body tense, from the muscles in her hands grasped by mine to the thigh alongside my own.

My tongue flicks out against her neck with my quiet chuckle. "I'm going to taste you now, Dayton. And I'm going to take my sweet fucking time exploring every bit of that beautiful cunt."

Her chest rises and falls frantically as I kiss down her neck and across the curve of her breasts. Her gorgeous, gorgeous tits that are begging to be held in my hands… Later. Right now, I can smell the wetness drenching what she calls panties, and it's calling to me.

My lips travel down her stomach to the curve of her hip and the turquoise string resting on it. There's nothing to these panties—fucking nothing at all—and I relish this. She picked these for me. She picked them because she knew I'd like the skimpy material that barely covers any of her.

I brush my finger across the material covering the mound above her folds and hook the tip beneath it.

"I like these. I hope you asked her for more than one pair."

I run my finger across the side and tug hard. The material frays then rips, falling away from her body and exposing the most intimate part of her to me the way it should be.

"Nope. Just that one."

"Order more." I lightly blow on her mound, smiling at the

shiver that runs through her body at the sensation. She pushes her hips forward in a silent beg for my mouth against her ready flesh.

I slowly run my hands across her thighs, savoring the silky feel of her skin beneath my palms, and hook her legs over my shoulders just like I once promised I would. I never break a fucking promise, especially not where Dayton and her pussy are concerned.

"Please," she whimpers, hooking her ankles behind my back.

I squeeze her tight ass, moving my mouth infinitesimally closer to her. "Are you begging?"

"No."

I run my nose along her thigh, pausing just before I reach the spot she's dying for me to touch her at.

"Are you begging?" I ask again, a hardness in my voice that demands a real answer.

"Yes," she gasps. "I'm fucking begging you!"

I stretch my tongue out and slowly run it across her slit, from her ass to the tip of her clit. I find her ready channel and flick my tongue inside it, her juices covering my tongue as I do. She tastes…

"Fuck," I moan, running my tongue along her again. I forgot this, this fucking incredible feeling of her against my mouth. "You taste amazing."

Her answering cry is music to my ears. I push her legs open even farther and continue my exploration of her pussy. She clenches her muscles beneath my fingertips and pushes her hips into my face. Small moans and cries fall repeatedly from between her lips, and I glance up.

Her eyes are closed, her lips parted. Her cheeks are flushed and rosy, and I can feel how close to the edge she is. I want to take her there. I want her to fall apart on my tongue.

"Dayton," I growl as I touch my thumb to her clit.

It has the desired effect as she explodes into my mouth and tugs on my hair and cries out loudly. I flex my tongue against her until she's calm, but her body is still quivering with the aftereffects of her orgasm when I lower her legs to my waist and stand.

Cupping her ass with my hand, I reach between us and position the end of my cock against her wet opening. The urge to slide inside her right now, to bury myself right to the hilt and feel her warmth around me is so strong. Instead, I hold back, teasing both of us with the gentle rubbing of my head against her.

"For the love of God, Aaron," Dayton breathes out, "just fuck me already!"

"You asked for it," I say as I close my lips over hers and push inside her with ease.

Her pussy walls clench around me, and it's like fucking heaven being inside her. Everything I remember and so, so much fucking more.

I push into her a second time and her pleasured shudder undoes me. I cup the back of her head, tilt her hips, and thrust into her harder and faster. Sweat covers our skin, and Dayton tightens her grip on my waist, allowing me to push even deeper inside her.

She reaches her fingers into my hair and grips hard, dropping her forehead to my shoulder. Every clench of her pussy brings me closer to the edge. Her high moans are my kryptonite, tightening my grasp on her body and deepening my thrusts inside her.

And I can feel it, the moment she holds back. The sharp intake of breath is too much.

"Stop fucking holding it back," I whisper into her ear. Her cunt clamps down on me, and my balls tighten as my own orgasm threatens. "Fuck. Dayton. Come. Now!"

She drops her head back, but that's not good enough. I want her looking into my fucking eyes so she remembers this moment. So she remembers that the person making her come isn't just a fucking client.

"Eyes. Look at me."

She moans, and they open briefly.

"Open your eyes!"

She does as I say this time, and I find myself lost in her dark, seductive gaze.

"Don't you dare close them. I want to see you and feel you come." I push deeper into her.

"Fuck," she whimpers.

"Hard. Come hard or not at all. Got it?"

She nods, and I take that as my cue. I pound into her, my cock reaching the very depths of her pussy, rubbing that sensitive spot over and over. I feel my cock swelling as her muscles tighten around me, and when I think she'll never come, she does.

She all but screams my name, tugging hard on my hair and squeezing my cock. The simultaneous action pulls my orgasm from me.

"God, Dayton," I groan into her neck, burying myself deep inside her as her muscles clench and pull everything she can from me.

She's shaking in my grip. Her whole body is quivering against me, and I kiss her to steady her. Her lips are warm as they sweep against mine, and I pull her from the wall.

Dayton pulls her hands from my hair and wraps her arms around my neck, hugging me close. I lower her to the bed, but she doesn't let go. Her arms stay firmly around me, and my cock is still inside her. I silence all the questions in my mind and spin us to the side.

I wrap my arms around her beautiful body and pull her against me. She snuggles into me, burying her face in my neck, and I close my eyes to a sigh leaving her lips. A sigh that sounds decidedly happy, I think.

I trail my fingers up and down her spine until, eventually, we both fall asleep.

The One Where The Truth Comes Out

I was raised to believe that every man has his own beliefs, whether you agree or not. I don't tend to agree with a lot of people.

I don't believe in God. I'm not religious, and I'm not convinced that there's a greater being out there, hovering above the clouds, watching my every move. That wasn't the family I was raised in.

But I sure as hell believe in fucking miracles, because nothing less could have brought Dayton Black back to me after seven long years.

I don't know what kind of luck was hanging over my head that day five weeks ago when she pulled that curtain shut and faced me. I wish I knew what fucked-up coincidence pulled us back together in a cruel yet beautiful twist of fate.

All I know is that she's here. And for now, she's mine.

I gently rub my thumb across her silky cheek, keeping my breathing shallow so I don't wake her. She looks so damn peaceful now, so damn beautiful. When she's sleeping like this, I know she's not worrying about us. She's not worrying about this ridiculous situation I keep forcing on her.

She's just being.

Her gorgeous tits are rising and falling with every breath she takes, and those pink lips I was nibbling on last night are parted ever so slightly. The urge to drop my mouth to hers and sweep her away in a sea of seduction is too much, too fucking much, so I pull my hand away from her face and roll over.

The bed creaks when I move, and I pause to look back at her. She doesn't move, deep in her slumber, and I stand. I grab some underwear and pants, tug them up my legs, and quietly leave the room. The door stands ajar behind me so I can hear her when she wakes.

'Cause, damn. I love her, but she's a real bitch until she's had her morning cup of coffee.

I fill the machine with extra coffee beans and water and turn it on. The low hum of it grinding the beans is an odd relaxant to me.

Spending so much time in London has lead me to prefer tea over coffee, if only just, but Dayton has reversed that. Her incessant need for "real caffeine," as she refers to it, is rubbing off on me slightly.

That, and she keeps me up all hours of the night with her wandering hands.

My phone buzzes from the kitchen counter where I left it last night, and I answer it without checking the caller ID.

"Aaron Stone."

"Son." My father's voice is tight yet warm, and I know instantly that he's calling with bad news. It's the middle of the fucking night in New York. "How are you?"

"Better than you, I assume, considering you're calling me at three a.m."

He takes a deep breath that makes the line crackle. "How is your time off?"

"What's the problem, Dad? It's eight in the morning and I don't have the time or patience to run through pleasantries."

"What makes you think something is wrong?"

"Twenty-seven years of life means I'm fairly well equipped to know when my father is keeping something from me." I walk across to the window and trace the outline of the Eiffel Tower the way I've watched Dayton do so many times. "Is there a problem with the business?"

"Not exactly."

"Then what, Dad?"

"Naomi."

I exhale harshly. Fuck. I knew she'd pop up somewhere. "What's she done this time?"

"Somehow she's discovered that you're in Paris and has taken it upon herself to organize a welcome dinner for you in your hotel."

A stream of curse words leaves my mouth. I'm not in the habit of swearing in front of my parents, but this situation calls for it.

"She's supposed to be in London. That's the entire reason for this week's break—to avoid a confrontation with her."

"I know, but she found out, and you're going have to attend this function."

"I'm not supposed to be working this week. You know that, Dad."

"I do, son. But the issue is that she's invited a lot of the Paris staff, including models and some clients. You understand the implications if you don't show your face."

"Yes." I run my fingers through my hair, every one of my muscles tightening with the prospect of coming face to face with my wife.

"You have to go, Aaron. Even if just for an hour. I take it Dayton isn't yet aware of Naomi?"

My jaw tightens, and I ignore his question. "Yes, we'll be there."

"Aaron, you must tell her."

"Okay. Bye." I hang up and let the phone fall from my fingers. It falls to the floor with a dense thud reminiscent of the way my heart dropped at the mention of my ex's name.

I fall onto the sofa and rest my arm across my eyes, sighing heavily. Fuck. This very situation is what I was trying to protect Day from.

"That doesn't sound like a great way to start your day." Her voice softly travels across the room, cutting through my thoughts.

"It's not!"

My voice is sharper than I meant, much sharper than she deserves. I can't help it. I know Naomi is hosting dinner tonight to spite me and prove some fucked-up point.

I lean my head back on the sofa and look at Dayton. She's hunched over the counter, a mug under the coffee machine. Defeat radiates from her the same way surprise does. I know I've never spoken to her that way.

She didn't deserve that.

I push off from the sofa and wrap my arms around her dainty waist. "Sorry. I shouldn't have spoken to you that way."

"Damn right you shouldn't have." She pours a cup of coffee, her chest jolting with a sharp breath. "Are you going to tell me what's wrong? If not, I'm going to shower."

I laugh quietly, trying to relieve some tension. Damn, she knows me so well. Too well, sometimes, I muse. "Someone I'm not particularly fond of heard we're in Paris this week. They've taken the liberty of organizing a company dinner here at the hotel tonight, and my father just informed me that we're expected to attend. Required to, actually."

"What if we had plans?" She steps from my loose hold and raises her eyebrows.

"We did." I lean against the counter with a heavy sigh. "Now we have new ones. Believe me. I'm not happy about it, Day."

"Can't you just explain you're not working this week? That this is a vacation?"

"No."

"Well, who is it?"

"Who?"

She clicks her tongue, an impatient, echoing sound. "The person organizing it."

"Oh. No one important. I'm not sure they'll even be there." I pour a cup of coffee, turning away so she won't see the alarm I know is in my eyes. Everything is going wrong. Just when it was so right, it's going wrong.

"Aaron," she pushes, her voice taking a hard tone I'm unused to.

"Leave it, Dayton." My words are equally as hard, and I hear the chink as her mug hits the marble kitchen counter I glance from the corner of my eye and watch her as she storms into the bedroom, her hips swinging tantalizingly as she does.

Fucking hell. She really shouldn't walk away from me when she's mad.

Ignoring the way my cock is hardening at the shake of her ass, I turn my thoughts back to the matter at hand. Can I convince Dayton that this is something I have to attend alone?

Unrealistic. She's not stupid. If I say that, she'll look right through me and laugh. I hired her to accompany me to shit like this. I can't exactly stop her doing so right now. No matter how inconvenient this is for me.

I have to try and cancel this, try and make it go away—my usual panic strategy. Surely my father can call the hotel and arrange some bullshit function to stop her dinner. His name has a lot more pull than hers does.

Dayton emerges from the bedroom, clad in figure-hugging workout gear. I fight the urge to run my eyes over her body and find her gaze, cold and seething.

"Look," I sigh, "I have a couple of calls to make now. Maybe you should go out for a couple of hours."

She grasps the door handle, her eyes never leaving mine. "I was planning to stay out all day. Don't worry."

"Day…"

She opens the door with an anger that belies her calm speech. "What time do you need me back here?"

"Four."

"Perfect. Don't bother calling me unless you've pulled your head from your ass and calmed the fuck down."

The door slams loudly behind her, shaking slightly, and I stare at it for a long moment. Fucking hell—this situation just went from bad to worse. Not only is my ex-wife, my dirty skeleton in my closet, stirring shit from her pathetic little rented Parisian apartment, my girlfriend, who knows nothing of her, is raging mad at me.

I take the coffee, retrieve my phone from the floor, and dial my father's number again.

Time for damage-control mode.

***

"Fucking hell!" I smack my hand against my forehead in defeat. I've spent nearly the last seven hours attempting to worm my way out of this ridiculous dinner—to no avail.

We have to go. That's the end of the story.

I have to tell Dayton the very thing I was keeping from her for her safety, and I have to do it soon. Before we get down there and she finds out from someone else. This isn't something anyone else has any right to tell her.

It's my secret and mine to tell.

Something I should have admitted long ago instead of paying her agent not to tell her.

I never thought my feelings toward this fiery brunette would be so strong after so long. I'll be the first to admit that she's always held my heart. Dayton Black has always been the one controlling the strings where my emotions are controlled, but I never realized that her control was so complete.

I had no idea she owned me so fucking entirely. I'm basically a pussy when it comes to admitting something so real.

Because, fuck, I wanted to tell her. I wanted to blurt it out every time she walked in a room or turned those gorgeous coffee-colored eyes on me. I wanted to rip my chest in two and bare my soul to her for her to do as she wished.

I still do.

But I know now that it won't be pretty.

Nothing good will come of our next conversation. Nothing will be salvaged.

I hope for a different outcome. Optimistically and perhaps naïvely, I hope.

She walks into the suite, the door clicking quietly behind her, and I find her stunning profile. She pauses but ignores me, turning toward the bedroom instead of speaking to me. Taking the easy way out.

I know all about taking the easy way out.

"Are you going to ignore me?" I ask, following her into the bedroom.

She drops the bag next to her suitcase and glances at the black dress I laid out earlier for her. "Are you going to talk to me like I deserve to be spoken to, or am I still your outlet for your annoyance?"

The pain that sneaks through into her voice cuts through me, and I walk to her. I fold her into my arms, bringing her close to my body, savoring the feel of her against me. "I'm sorry, sweetheart. I was wrong to take it out on you."

"Fucking right you were." She wraps her arms around my waist and rests her head against my chest. My heart thumps beneath her ear. "Don't do it again."

"Ever?"

"*Ever.* Next time I won't be so nice to you, nor will I walk away. Talk to me like crap again, Mr. Stone, and I'm going to tear you a new asshole. Got it?"

I bend down, bringing my mouth close to hers. "Got it," I whisper, taking her sweet lips with mine.

This could be the last time I kiss her. I linger on that thought, unwilling to let the kiss break. Damn if I don't need this woman.

"Are you going to tell me who has you in a bad mood yet?" Dayton pulls away, flicking her hair over her shoulder, and tugs her sports bra over her head. My cock twitches at the blue bra she slips on, more so when she adjusts her tits inside it.

"Someone from my past who delights in making my life incredibly hard." I discard my shirt on the chair and take a freshly laundered one from the closet, sliding it over my shoulders. I button it up, focusing on them instead of her. I'm a fucking coward. "If there were a way to get out of this tonight, you can bet I'd find it."

"Wow. I can't imagine disliking someone that much." Dayton steps into the dress and reaches behind her, struggling with the zipper. "Who is it?"

I step up to her and knock her hand away. With my fingers clasped around the zipper pull, I slide it upward smoothly and take a deep breath. I know this is it.

This could be the last time I get to brush my fingers against her skin, get to touch her, get to be anywhere fucking near her.

"Aaron?" she repeats, apprehension tingeing her tone.

I take a second deep breath and close my eyes resignedly. "The person organizing tonight is my wife."

The One Where She Walks Away

She moves from me suddenly, her sharp jump a punch in my gut. *It's what you were expecting,* I remind myself. *I knew this would happen.*

"Wife?" Her voice is barely more than whisper, tinged with accusation and disbelief. Her hands are clasped in front of her slightly bent-over body, shaking so discreetly that no one but I would ever notice it.

But I do. I know her so fucking well my next word cuts as much as the last seven did.

"Yes."

She covers her mouth with her hand, turning away from me with closed eyes. Jesus. I can feel the pain emanating from her and wrapping around me in a suffocating blanket. Fuck. I can't feel this—the pain I'm causing her. I have to explain, to somehow justify my decision to keep her a secret.

"She's my ex-wife, actually. We'd be divorced if she didn't keep stalling on the agreement," I ramble, my eyes following her.

"You're still married. She's still your wife."

"We've been separated for two years."

She shakes her head, her eyes still closed. "And you never thought to tell me?"

"I didn't know how to. I kept putting it off until it became impossible. I wanted to, Day." I move to her and gently rest my hands on her arms. Shit. I wish she'd understand. I need her to fucking understand why I didn't tell her!

"Don't you dare touch me." Her voice is hard when she steps away. A pang hits my chest when she rubs her hands across her arms where mine just were. Rubbing my touch away. "Don't you fucking dare stand there in front of me and try and justify this. Shit, Aaron. You're married! Fucking *married!*"

Her eyes open, and in them, I see pure contempt. Anger. Disbelief. A sliver of hatred that hurts more than the prospect of losing her.

"Didn't she sit still long enough for you to work your shit out, huh? So much for making sure you'd work it out. Fuck! All that was a lie, wasn't it? How much more has been a lie? How many more lines have you said that actually mean fucking nothing?"

"Our marriage was a sham, Dayton. Naomi cares for nothing but money and fame. She was an up-and-coming model struggling to break into the industry. I met her one night at college and could see her potential, so I gave her the in. I set her up with one of our agents, and she was…thankful." I rub my forehead. Lamest fucking excuse in the world.

"I bet she was."

"We started seeing each other casually, and every time I went to break it off, my father's assistant convinced me it was good for us to be together because of our profiles. Our 'relationship' was no secret, and she was always being hit with the fact that she'd only made it because of me."

"She did!"

"We both knew that. I was a buffer for that. I claimed we met after she signed with our agency and that was that."

"And you woke up one morning and decided to marry her, right? Because it was the 'right' thing to do?" She raises her eyebrows and storms past me.

I sigh heavily. "It didn't work out. After eight months, we separated. I've been fighting her for two years. She's not entitled to half of everything I own, but she won't take what I am offering. There's a reason I don't own the company on paper yet."

"I can't even look at you right now. I can't believe you didn't tell me about her. How couldn't you tell me, Aaron? Did it not ever cross your mind while you were watching me sleep or pouring me coffee to tell me? How about when you were kissing me or fucking me? Or when you were writing little fucking notes and hiding them?!"

I finally find her eyes again and hope my gaze can show her everything I feel. "I was so scared to lose you, Day. So scared that if I told you, you'd get up and walk and that would be that."

"So you thought you'd ignore it and she'd go away eventually? That I'd never find out? Even when you were begging me to move in with you—did you really think then that you'd never have to tell me?" She closes her eyes and pushes her fingers into them, and even I can tell she's fighting tears.

"I hoped I could call my lawyer and give her what she wants from our marriage. My money. Then yes, I hoped she'd go away. I had no idea she was in France right now. If I did, I never would have brought us here."

"What a nice surprise that was. No wonder you couldn't tell me this morning."

I step forward, her sharp words slicing through every part of me. I deserve it. I deserve every fucking word she throws at me. "I'm so sorry, Dayton. If you had to find out, it never should have been like this. I'm so sorry."

"Believe me, Aaron. You're not half as sorry as I am." She turns and disappears into the bathroom.

I stare at the doorway for a moment. I have no words for this situation, for this utter fuck-up I've caused. Once again, I berate myself for doing what I assumed would protect her.

I follow her into the bathroom, and upon finding her in front of the mirror with her makeup bag, I pause. "What are you doing?"

I can see it happen. The moment she meets my eyes in the mirror, I know I'm not looking at Dayton. I'm looking at Mia, the woman she was always supposed to be with me.

"I have a contractual obligation to fill. I'll be there with you tonight, but I'm leaving right after," she replies simply.

I draw in a sharp breath. Leaving? No. Fuck no.

"You'll be refunded for the final two weeks that will be unfulfilled. Then you will wipe my agent's number from your phone and not contact her again. I'll be changing mine when I'm back in Seattle."

"Day, please—"

"My other option is leaving right now and letting your wife

know she's got between us. I'll leave late tonight and use the company plane. This way you can tell everyone I had a family emergency and had to return home immediately." She coats her lips in red lipstick and rubs them together before continuing. "We both have reputations to protect, and that's exactly what I'm doing."

She strolls past me as I take in her words.

A few hours. That's all I have. All I have to try and right this major fucking wrong. I don't have a clue where to begin, but I know I can't take that cold, impersonal stare. I don't give a shit if I fucking deserve it. I don't want it.

I follow her into the kitchen. "Don't look at me with Mia's eyes."

I knot my tie and shrug my jacket on while she pours a glass of wine and drains some of it in one long drink. Slowly, she turns to me, her face blank, her eyes expressionless, her hands perfectly still.

"I'm doing my job, Aaron. You're my client. That's it."

***

I don't know how she can be so composed.

To look at her, you wouldn't believe she'd been crying not half an hour ago. Her eyes are bright, even if I can see the ache lingering in the depths of them, and her mouth is curved in a false smile as we enter the room.

And this whole thing is fucking stupid. This dinner, this charade. I want to take this woman standing next to me back upstairs, sit her down, and make her listen to me. I have no clue what I can say to attempt to make this better. There's a high chance I'd just make it worse, but I have to do something.

I can't let her walk away from me tonight.

I won't let her.

Not again. Not this time.

"Aaron! How lovely for you to clear your schedule for tonight," Naomi declares in a shrill voice.

I pull myself from my thoughts and stare at my ex-wife. Her blond hair is as fake as ever, her eyelashes too long to be real, and the glimmer of viciousness in her eyes pushes every one of my buttons.

What the hell possessed me to marry her?

"I believe I had no choice," I respond dryly. "Dayton, this is Naomi. My ex-wife." I wave my hand between them. "Naomi, my girlfriend, Dayton."

"Oh, I've heard so much about you!" Naomi fakes a smile and leans forward to air-kiss Dayton.

She returns it in the most controlled display I've ever seen in my life. Every woman I know would be clawing her eyes out—but not my Dayton. She puts on a smile and does exactly what she knows will rile Naomi.

"Really?" Dayton replies, stepping back into my side. "I can't say I've heard very much about you at all. A few passing comments, maybe."

My lips twitch as I fight my smile.

Naomi blinks. "Oh. I suppose Aaron's been very busy with taking over the company and you haven't had much time to talk."

"Oh, we've had plenty of time to talk...among other things... but you just never came up." Dayton leans into me with a demure smile.

Naomi's jaw visibly tightens, her eyes filling with mirth, and she doesn't respond. Instead, she turns to me. "And how is the change going?"

"The contracts are locked in the lawyer's desk, waiting for the day our divorce papers land there." I feel the twitch of my fingers at Dayton's side. Our relationship isn't something I wanted to revisit tonight, no matter how inevitable it was. "We can all hope that will be soon."

"Oh, darling. You're being unreasonable in your agreement. Can't we just discuss it?"

"Naomi, you made a point by organizing this tonight. If you found out I'm here, I'm sure you're aware I'm not working this week. I don't wish to discuss anything with you. I'm not paying two lawyers so we can sit and have coffee to iron out your ridiculous terms."

Dayton turns her body into me and rests her hand against my stomach. "Aaron, honey," she says in a soft voice. "Shall we get a drink? I don't think this is the place to be discussing this."

I stare at Naomi for a long moment before I turn away and kiss Dayton's temple. "You're right. Let's go."

We leave Naomi standing alone and cross to the bar. I can feel Dayton wanting to pull away from me, feel her fighting to stay close. It only makes me hold her tighter.

"You handled her well." I hand her a glass of wine and sip my own drink.

"Nothing like letting the woman your boyfriend is married to think you don't care." She flicks her tongue out across her bottom lip and raises her glass to her mouth, her eyes finding mine coldly. "She's a bitch, by the way. You picked a real good one there."

Didn't I? A good one who, through my own stupidity, has ruined the only real good relationship I've ever had in my life. The only one that's ever really meant anything.

Dayton's eyes flick between her glass and Naomi. I wonder if she even realizes she's doing it. I wonder if she can feel her heart breaking the way I can see it in her eyes.

I wonder if the guilt in my eyes reflects the consuming feel of it inside.

Dayton puts her glass down and reaches inside her purse. "Excuse me. I have a call."

What?

No. Fucking no.

She turns away from me and walks through the room, her cell against her ear and her purse tucked under her arm so she can put her finger in her other ear. It's good, I'll give her that. Convincing. If I didn't know what this meant.

I discard my drink on the bar and follow her, ignoring Naomi's eyes on my back. Fuck her. All that matters now is Dayton and stopping her from leaving.

The elevators doors close on me, and I curse under my breath, looking at the second elevator. I press the down button repeatedly, knowing that it'll get down three floors faster than I can climb twenty sets of stairs.

The doors open and I run in without a care for anyone else. I pace the tiny space as it climbs the floors, rubbing my hand through my hair. Fuck fuck fuck.

The second it dings on my floor, I run out of it and into our suite door. I fumble for the key in my pocket, slide the card through, and shove the door open.

I find her eyes immediately, like my own are drawn to her dark gaze.

"Yes," she says into the phone. "He's aware."

I draw in a sharp breath. "Don't go." My voice comes out as a whisper. "Please. Don't go."

"I don't have a choice." She zips her cases with a calmness that contradicts the shaking of her hands. "If you'd told me before, maybe I could have dealt with it. But to tell me an hour before you expect me to stand face to face to her? No way, Aaron. No way."

"Dayton. Please." I'm aware of the plea in my voice. Fuck. I'd get on my knees and beg if it meant she would stay here. With me. I cross the room swiftly and cup her face in my hands. Her cheeks are like silk against my palms as I bring my forehead to hers. "Please. Just one night. Let me explain everything. Just don't leave me again."

"You knew I was going tonight. I'm just leaving sooner. I can't stay down there with her, and it's ridiculous to expect me to."

I see the tears before I register the crack of her voice. They hurt more than anything. Fuck a punch to the gut—watching the woman I love so much cry is like being hit with a freight train and crushed by its weight.

"Fuck, Dayton," I rasp, my own emotion evident in my voice, and I brush my thumb under her eyes to wipe away the wetness. "Don't go, baby. Don't go."

She takes a deep breath and steps back. My hands fall to my sides limply, and she shakes her head. "You lied to me, Aaron. A lie of omission, but a lie all the same. This isn't a tiny thing that can be swept under the rug and forgotten. This is huge and a central part of your life. All the times you asked me to tell you everything about me, you were never willing to return that. You were never going to tell me. You said so yourself. I can't stay. I'm sorry."

She swipes at her cheeks, and all I can do is stare at her. Every part of me is screaming to reach out to her, to grab her, to hold her to me and never let her go.

There's a knock at the door and she opens it, sniffing quietly. A porter is standing there, a cart at his side, and my chest tightens. She opens the door wider for him to enter, and all I can do is stand in silence as he loads her suitcases onto the cart and pushes it back outside the room.

"Is my car ready?" Dayton asks quietly.

"*Oui, mademoiselle.*" He disappears into the lift, and she grasps the doorknob tighter.

"I'm begging you, Dayton. I'm fucking begging you not to go."

"I was ready to give it all up," she whispers, her voice cracking. "When you gave me my necklace again, I was going to tell you. I was ready to give it all up to be with you. I was going to call Monique, cancel the payment, and leave her. I didn't think I could walk away from you again. I didn't know if I'd survive another broken heart."

Her words ricochet through me so fucking painfully that I can barely breathe. "So don't. Stay. *Please.*"

"You were right. True love never dies. It only fades, lingering below the surface until we're ready for it again. Until fate puts us in the right place and the right time and that simmering love can come alive again." She clasps her purse to her chest and looks over her shoulder at me. "I love you, Aaron, but I have more integrity than to stay with a man who can lie to me so easily. I respect myself too much. I'm sorry. I can't stay."

She runs through the doors, and I move instinctively. Her words fuel my running toward the elevator. Just in time to see the doors close.

"Day! Fuck, Dayton!"

I slam my hands against the doors. My chest is heaving as her words repeat again in my mind.

"*I love you, Aaron...*"

I push off from the doors and head toward the stairwell. Fuck this. I need to get down there to her. I need to try one last time. I don't care that I look like a madman in an expensive suit, flying down the stairs of Paris's most exclusive hotel. All I care about is getting to the woman who has held my heart for seven years.

But I'm too late. I explode into the lobby and my eyes find her car immediately as the door closes. It pulls away from the hotel and leaves me standing in the middle of the lobby, unable to do anything but watch her go.

I'm powerless. This is a situation I'm unable to control, one I was never able to.

I run my fingers through my hair, anger mixing with the dull ache in my chest, and I turn to the concierge. "Do you have anywhere I can make a private call?"

"*Oui*. Follow me, sir." He leads me to a small room off the lobby and leaves me.

I pull out my cell and dial my assistant's number. She answers immediately.

"Aaron Stone's office. How may I help you?"

"Dottie, it's me."

"Oh, Mr. Stone! Is everything all right?"

"No, honestly. I need you to do something for me."

"Of course." I hear the shuffle of papers as she grabs her notepad and pen. "What is it?"

"Cancel all my meetings next week and the next. Condense as many of the Paris meetings into the next seven days. If they can't do it, then tough. I will be leaving Paris at six p.m. on the twenty-third. Got that?"

"Yes. Anything else?"

"Call Mr. Carlisle Sr. in New York and request that he draw up new divorce papers. Seven and a half is my final offer. I'll be flying back to New York."

"Absolutely. Mr. Stone…are you okay?"

I exhale loudly and rub my fingers through my hair. "Not particularly, Dottie, but there's nothing I can do in this moment. Email me a schedule by tomorrow morning. Goodbye."

I pocket my phone and leave the tiny space, my eyes set on the room we were just in. Naomi approaches me as soon as I walk through the door.

"Oh, Aaron. You almost missed dinner. Oh, where is your girlfriend?" Her smirk is anything but concerned.

I wrap my fingers around her arm and tug her from the room and back to the space I just called Dottie from. Then I slam the door behind us and pin her with my angry stare.

"I have no idea what you're playing at with this tonight, Naomi, but it's ridiculous. You're not in high school anymore. Our relationship is over, and it never should have begun."

"She didn't know about us, did she?"

"What Dayton did or didn't know is irrelevant and, quite frankly, none of your business. What is your business is the fact I will be returning to New York in seven days. My lawyer is drawing up new divorce papers now, and understand this." I put my hands on the small table between us and lean forward. "You will fucking sign them. It's my final offer and more than you deserve. If you refuse to sign them, we'll take it to court and you'll get less."

Her face whitens despite her effort to remain composed. And why wouldn't it? She's being threatened out of money. Money she has no entitlement to.

"Let's not be hasty, now—"

"Hasty?" I shout. "You've been playing this bullshit game for two years, and I'm finished. I'm done, Naomi. You'll be flown to New York when I've looked over the papers to sign. There will be no further dancing around each other's lawyers. There will be no more pushing unnecessarily. Do you understand me?"

She clicks her tongue and nods harshly.

"Good. Now if you'll excuse me, I'm going to retire for the evening." I stand, adjust my jacket, and move toward the door. "I won't be attending dinner tonight. I have far more important issues to attend to. Pass on my apologies to the others."

I leave the room before she can respond and slip into a waiting elevator. I lean back against the mirrored wall, a heaviness settling over me from knowing that I'm returning to an empty room.

I could chase her. I could call the pilot and have him hold the plane until I get there.

But I can't. I'm not letting her go, but I'm not rushing it either. Before I get her back, I have to figure everything out. I have to end this sham of a marriage properly, take care of a bit of business, then relocate to Seattle.

Then, and only then, can I fight for Dayton.

I hold on to this thought as I enter the suite that still smells so much like her.

The One Where He Makes Arrangements

I wearily let myself into my apartment. Seven days of nonstop meetings and a long flight—not to mention the time change—have done a number on me. There's nothing I'd like more than to step out of these jeans and T-shirt and climb into bed for a large number of hours.

But as the screen of my cell lights up with my mother's number flashing on screen, I know that isn't an option until later tonight.

"Mom," I answer, rubbing my forehead.

"Mr. Carlisle will be waiting for you with your divorce papers at nine a.m. at the house. If you feel like you can drag yourself over here to look at them, please do." She hangs up without another word.

Actually, after those two sentences, I don't feel like dragging myself over there at all. Hearing my mother's less-than-pleasant inner thoughts out loud is never enjoyable, especially not when they involve my ex and are directed at me. Nevertheless, I should have expected this.

I also know that her last sentence was her attempting to be polite. What she really meant was that, if I have any brain cells at all, I better get my ass over there before the lawyer shows.

I step into the bathroom for a quick shower, trying not to think about the last time I did this alone. Usually there's another person in here for me to run my hands over, to kiss, to wash. And usually, that person is doing the same thing back to me…

I exhale deeply, washing the soap from my body. God, I miss her. If I thought Dayton's leaving me seven years ago was painful, I wasn't prepared for this. I wasn't prepared for the hollow feeling inside my chest or every lackluster beat of my heart.

Her laugh, her smile, the twinkle she gets in her eyes every time I look at her… I miss it all, and it's only been a matter of days. I didn't realize just how much I love her until I watched that car pull away from the hotel, taking her with it.

I didn't realize just how much brighter she makes life.

I dress quickly, tugging a jacket over my sweater, and push my cell into my pocket. It rings again, and I'm relieved to see Dad's name on the screen.

"Dad."

"Your mom would like to know if you're on your way yet."

My eyes drift to the clock on the wall. "Yes, I'm about to leave.

Forty-five minutes earlier than necessary."

He relays this message to her, and a heavy breath crackles down the phone as he brings it back to his ear. "She says not to be smart, and she hopes you arrive with a little more respect than you're currently showing her."

Twenty-seven years old and the woman can still make me feel like a kid.

"I'll try my best," I reply.

"He said he's sorry. He's simply tired after his long flight, and he'll make sure to bring a better attitude," Dad calls. A door shuts, and he exhales. "Good grief. Son, she's not happy."

"Really, Dad? I wasn't aware from our earlier conversation." I get into the waiting car with a nod to the building doorman.

"I hope you have plenty of medication in your apartment, because I suspect you'll need it when you leave. Although, I have to say, at this point, rather you than me."

I wince. I can just imagine what he's had to put up with for the last few days. To the public eye, my mother is the walking embodiment of composure and elegance, even when angry. In private, she's the exact opposite.

Quite frankly, it makes me want to turn this car around and have Mr. Carlisle email a copy of the agreement instead.

"I'll be there in a few minutes." I end the call and lean back on the seat.

An endless tirade over my shortcomings with my first marriage and choice of wife isn't what I planned for this morning.

The drive through New York is more painful than I remember, likely because I've been spoiled by quieter cities over the past month. When I finally arrive at my parents' house, I linger in the car for a few minutes.

Unfortunately, my mother appears at the front door, meaning my attempts at prolonging the beginning of our conversation are thwarted.

"Inside," she barks, her eyes hard and disappointed.

I bite my tongue. I know better than to respond to her in this mood...most of the time. Occasionally, the words slip out.

She points at the front room, and I walk in, dutifully taking a seat on the sofa. My father lowers his paper at a sharp look from Mom and glances at me with sympathy in his eyes.

Oh yes. This is going to be bad.

Mom looks at me for a long moment, her eyes shining with anger, before sighing resignedly. She reaches behind her head and secures her hair up with a large clip then brings her attention back to me.

"Why, Aaron? Why didn't you tell her?"

I open my mouth, but she carries on, and I realize that all of her questions will be rhetorical until she decides otherwise. Perils of having a mother who is used to dealing with men like my father... and me.

"I don't understand why it was so difficult. What were you trying to protect her from? The truth? Impossible. You can't protect people from the truth with lies, openly said or otherwise. If it were any other girl...fine. But Dayton isn't just anyone." She sighs and puts her hands on her hips, and she's gaining the steam she lost a moment ago. "You should have foreseen this. You should have expected that bitch—"

"Carly!"

"Shut up, Brandon!" she snaps without looking Dad's way. "You should have expected her to pull a stunt like this. She despises Dayton without having met her. Your past with her is what held you back in that godforsaken relationship with that little gold-digger. The second she got wind of you being in Paris with her, she rushed over from London with a samurai sword to stab you in the back, and you damn well let her because of your stupidity."

"Come on now, Mom. I was doing what I thought was best!" I sit up straight.

She raises her eyebrows. "And one day you will learn that mother knows best. I told you to be honest with that girl, and you didn't. Now look. What do you have to show for it?"

I rub my hand across my forehead, feeling a dull throb beginning behind my eyes. "Can we discuss this another day? I'm exhausted and would like to get this meeting done with so I can go back to bed. I'd also like to wait in peace."

"No, Aaron, we can't discuss it another day."

"Carly, give him a little break. He's had it rough."

"Of his own making!" Mom looks at him this time, and my father visibly shrinks. Behold the power of a woman's stare. She spins her eyes back to me. "What are you going to do to solve this mess? Obviously divorcing Naomi is the smartest move you've made in a long time, but how much is that costing you? How much are you losing just to put an end to that sham you called a marriage?"

"Enough, Mother."

"And then what? Are you going to jet to Seattle and expect Dayton to take you back because you snap your fingers? I wouldn't put it past you. That's exactly what your father would do. But it won't work, Aaron. You won't be able to show up and have her fall for it all over again. And even then, do you really expect Naomi to let it lie? She works for the company!"

"I said enough!" I yell, standing quickly. "In case it escaped your notice, I'm more than aware of the situation I'm in. Divorcing Naomi will cost me seven and a half million or it goes to court, something she knows. In the grand scheme of things, seven million really isn't a lot. As for her working for us, that's something I plan to rectify before the ink is even dry on the business contracts. And Dayton… I haven't considered that yet. I know you're doing this because you care, but this discussion is now over."

The doorbell rings, and I walk into the office, ready to meet Mr. Carlisle and look over the papers. Mom follows me, her heels clicking against the floor.

"What do you mean you plan to rectify Naomi working for us? Aaron! Aaron!"

"Should I come back later?" Mr. Carlisle stands in the doorway of the office, next to my father.

"Absolutely not, Stephen. Carly is just fussing," Dad answers. "Carly, darling, we could use some coffee."

In a role reversal, he pins her with a severe gaze. Any other woman would melt into the wall in fear, but not her. She merely clicks her tongue, throws a cursory, annoyed glance my way that says we're not done here, and stalks from the room.

Collectively, we three men exhale. Dad shuts the door behind her and motions for Mr. Carlisle to lay the papers out on the desk.

"Let's get on with this," I say. "I'd like to leave before she returns. I think she shaved ten years off my age somewhere during the last few days, and I'm even less fond of her rages now than I was then."

Mr. Carlisle smiles. He's more than aware of my mother's... ways. "The only change I made was the monetary amount as you requested, Aaron. Everything else, including the no-contact clause, is as it was."

I run my eyes over the sheets of paper in front of me, barely reading the words, and nod once. "Dad, how soon can we get her flown over here?"

"Likely on the next flight—if she'll come."

"She will," I respond confidently, leaning forward to get the phone. I dial the Seattle office number, getting Dottie. "Dottie. Can you check the next flight from CDG in Paris to JFK for Naomi?"

"I'll call you back in five minutes." The phone clicks off, and I set mine back in the holder.

"Efficient assistant you have there," Mr. Carlisle remarks.

"Only the best."

The phone rings within the five-minute frame she gave me and I smile.

"There's a flight leaving at eight a.m., Paris time. She'll land here late tonight ready for a meeting for you tomorrow."

"Perfect. Book that flight in her name."

"Class?"

"Economy. And book her a hotel room…somewhere. Make sure the airline knows that the fee will be paid upon her collection of the tickets."

I can almost hear her smiling down the phone. "Very well, sir. And the hotel room?"

"You don't need me to answer that, do you, Dottie?"

"I'll get right on it." She hangs up on me for a second time.

I turn my head and find my father staring at me, a bemused look on his face. "What?"

"Economy class? God, son. She'll have a fit."

I shrug a shoulder, dialing my ex's number. "I have to get my kicks somewhere, Dad. Besides, it'll improve Mom's mood somewhat."

I redial four times before Naomi finally answers with a snap. "Do you know what time it is?"

"I do," I respond. "And you should look at it, because you have a flight to catch in four hours."

"Excuse me?" I hear movement down the line.

"A flight. To New York."

"You'll find that I don't, Aaron."

"You'll find that you do, Naomi. Dottie will be emailing you your flight details any time."

"You can't just book me a flight and expect me to jump on it."

"Absolutely, I can. Because if you aren't on this flight today and you aren't in my office at ten tomorrow morning to sign the papers sitting in front of me, you won't be signing them at all and we'll be settling this in court. This is your final chance, Naomi."

"You're a fucking asshole, Aaron Stone."

"You don't know the half of it." I set the phone back in the holder, effectively ending the call, and straighten. Both Mr. Carlisle and my father are watching me with matching looks that tell of their hidden laughter. "If you'll excuse me, Dad, Mr. Carlisle, I'm going home to bed. That flight last night was a bastard."

"What about your mother?" Dad calls after me.

I open the front door and wave a hand over my shoulder. "Tell her about the economy flight and I'm sure she'll forgive me."

The One Where He Gets Divorced

I woke six times during my jet-lag nap, each time stretching my hand out across the bed to reach for a woman who wasn't there. Even now, I pull two coffee mugs from the cupboard, and it takes me until after I've filled them both to remember why I don't need the second.

It's a dull throb, knowing she's not here. It's not a crippling, intense pain that comes in waves, peaking every now and then. It's a constant ache, not enough to stop me from going about my business, but enough that I'm always aware of it. Enough to be a sucker-punch in the gut here and there.

It hits the most when I think about her. Then, the ache intensifies into a full-body sweep of longing. Through the longing is the guilt. That is, for me, perhaps the worst part of this situation. Knowing there's the chance that it could have been avoided, that I could have done something about it if only I'd been brave enough at the start.

It's the guilt that I not only caused this and hurt myself but hurt her in the process. That's the biggest portion of it. Seeing that teary sheen to her eyes as they filled with wetness and the subtle quiver of her bottom lip as she held in her emotions haunts me every time I close my eyes. The sound of her voice as she spoke to me accusingly, speaking the way I deserved to be spoken to, echoes in my ears whenever I'm surrounded by silence.

The last thing I ever wanted to do was hurt her, and I did it while trying to do the opposite. That fact doesn't escape me.

I finish the last of my coffee, tightly closing my eyes as the hot liquid burns my throat, and shrug my jacket on. My car is waiting for me downstairs, and I climb in, flipping through my calendar on my phone.

I meant to see my schedule to see what I have coming up in an attempt to rid my mind from the woman currently possessing it, but instead I'm seeing how soon I can leave New York. How quickly I can return to Seattle to set this whole thing straight.

Two days, realistically. That's two days too long. I can possibly leave tomorrow, but that's pushing it. Still, though...

Leaving Dayton in a city on the other side of the country for much longer, without me, is unfathomable. Regardless of how hard I may have to fight to win her back, I can't fight if I'm not there.

Tomorrow it is.

I stroll into the office and up the elevator without a word to anyone. My pending divorce aside, I've been preparing for today for as long as I can remember. Four years of studying for a business degree, interning here, summer jobs filing—they were all for today, the moment my father signs the business over to me.

It's insane, and slightly overwhelming, to think that this empire he's built will belong to me when I walk out of this building.

I rap twice on his office door and step inside. He's already waiting with my mother, the lawyer, and my cousin, Tyler. Tyler slaps me on the back of my shoulder, but my focus is on the desk and the files sitting in front of Mr. Carlisle.

The phone rings and my father presses the button on the set. "Yes?"

"Ms. Lane is here to see you, sir."

"Send her in." He ends the connection and stands, motioning for me to take a seat behind the desk.

My eyebrow quirks at him, but all he does is reinforce the motion. I do as he silently requests and lower myself into the plush leather chair he's offering.

Naomi enters the room with her usual self-righteousness. She winks at Tyler, and he responds with a disgusted look. She's not exactly popular, even with my womanizing cousin.

"Ms. Lane." Mr. Carlisle greets her and holds out one of the seats opposite the desk. "I trust you're aware of the purpose of today's meeting?"

Naomi turns steely eyes on me. "Perfectly aware. Thank you."

"Then let's get on with it." I slide the file forward. "Nothing in it has changed, just the amount, but feel free to read through it so you're satisfied."

She takes the file without looking at me and flips through it, sighing when she reaches the page with the amount. She doesn't contest, just like I knew she wouldn't, and hands the file back to me after several minutes.

"You win, Aaron. Sign it and pass it back."

I flip to the marked pages and scrawl my signature on each dictated line, a sense of freedom washing over me as I do. Naomi does the same when I hand it back to her, finality settling over her features.

"Excellent," I mutter, taking my pen back from her. I turn to the lawyer. "And the other?"

He hands me the business contracts wordlessly. I have no need to read these. I've read them more times than my divorce papers, and I know that my father and Mr. Carlisle have already signed them because I asked them to in advance.

Naomi stands as I flick through another set of marked pages and I hold my finger up, indicating she should wait. I hear her heavy sigh as she does and continue my signatures on the hefty contract. When I reach the end, I close the file and set the pen on top.

My eyes meet Naomi's as I stand. Silence weighs heavily in the room, anticipation and curiousness threading through it as my family and our legal representative look on.

"Yes?" Naomi responds in a bored tone.

I adjust my cuff link, breaking our eye contact for a moment before I find her gaze once more. I have to control my smirk as the words roll off my tongue.

"I'm afraid your modeling services are no longer required at the Stone Agency. Your agent is aware and in full agreement, and you may stop by her office on your way out to collect any details she may have and any possible future contracts should you decide to pursue a new agent outside of the company."

Her mouth opens and closes several times until she resembles a fish. She straightens in her heels and looks at me furiously. "You're firing me?"

"Firing you, letting you go… Call it what you will, Ms. Lane, but we will no longer be representing you."

"You can't do that! This is unfair dismissal."

I rest my hands on the large antique desk in front of me and meet her eyes so she knows I'm being serious. "You haven't signed a major contract in fifteen months, and since then, you've had less than ten jobs of any caliber. I'm letting you go on account of my belief that your time in this industry is coming to an end, and your former agent agrees with me, as do the director and manager of the agency. If you care to dispute our reasoning, then you are more than welcome. Until then, we're done here. You know the way out."

I sit down, tearing my eyes from hers and ignoring the harsh bark of laughter from my cousin. Naomi lingers for a moment, her eyes flicking over everyone in the room, then turns and leaves. The door slams behind her, and I finally give in to the twitch of my lips.

"Well, that's soothed the sting a little," Mom remarks casually. "Nothing like some early morning entertainment, especially when she is the victim." She pats me on the shoulder.

"Was all that true?" Mr. Carlisle questions me. "If not, she can take you to court."

"It's true," Dad clarifies. "I've been considering terminating her contract for a couple of months now, but in light of recent events, I decided I would let Aaron do the honors."

"If you believe she'll contest our claims, I'll have the agency staff send you a full list of her contracts from the last two years," I offer Mr. Carlisle. "I'd rather we cover all bases. She can be vindictive."

Tyler snorts behind me but keeps his words to himself.

"Yes, best you do." Mr. Carlisle stands and puts the files in his briefcase. "I will see to it that these find their rightful homes and that copies are returned to you, Mr. Stone. Junior," he adds as an afterthought.

I smile and stand to shake his hand. "Thank you, Mr. Carlisle. You've been incredibly helpful."

"Just doing my job." He turns to my father, shakes his hand, and subsequently kisses my mother's cheek before leaving.

I sit down for a second time and exhale deeply. This business now belongs to me, and Naomi is no longer a thorn in my side. Now all that's left to do is—

"When are you going to get her?" Tyler asks.

"Tomorrow."

EMMA HART

The One Where He Finds Her At The Club

Light rain beats against the windows of my Seattle apartment. I stand in the front room, against the ceiling-high windows, and look out at the city.

I've been here so many times, and every time, I've looked and wondered where she was. Seven weeks ago, I got my answer. She was standing in front of me in a hotel looking so fucking beautiful that it hurt.

I vowed, there and then, that I'd never let her go again. That the only time I'd see her waking away from me would be because she'd be walking into the bedroom, ready for me to follow her. Or perhaps into the kitchen wearing nothing but my shirt, ready to make coffee.

I broke my promise to myself and my promise to her, but now,

I'm determined to make it right again.

No matter how hard it is. I need my woman back in my life, and this time, I need her to stay.

My cell buzzes with a message from Tyler telling me that he's back in London and he thinks there's a possibility that the woman he fucked last night works for me. Fantastic. Not that I'm surprised any. While I spent my teen years pushing my father to teach me everything he knows about running a business, Tyler was gaining enough experience with girls to manage a porn company and give the girls real orgasms to boot.

I drop it on the bar in my kitchen and pour some whisky in a glass, barely glancing at the measurement. It burns my throat as it goes down, but it's a welcome burn, and the subsequent warmth spreads through my body.

To know that Dayton is here, in this city, is making my body hum with anticipation and fear. I know she's here, just not where… If she's working or not.

Fuck. If she's working. I don't believe it, not in my heart, but the chill she looked at me with in Paris when she informed me that I was just her client is enough to make me doubt it. If she can be so impersonal and emotionally blank standing right in front of me, surely she can do it without me being around.

My cell buzzes again, and I look at the ceiling. If that's Tyler…

She's in Vibe.

I stare at Uncle Ted's text. We own a handful of bars and clubs together, mainly in Seattle, but I leave the running of them to him while my aunt manages the restaurant side. The nightlife has never really been my thing, but the business opportunity came up. Working with my uncle was a no-brainer, even five years ago.

And now I know where she is. In the first bar we bought together, the one that doubles as a nightclub. Vibe Bar. The one a block away from my apartment.

I run my fingers through my hair. The temptation to go down there and see her, even if we don't talk, is so strong. It would take me a minute to get there.

I want to see her. I fucking need to see her, to see if she's okay, who she's with...

Who is she with?

A blond girl.

I nod my head, letting my breath out. Good. That's probably her best friend, Liv. I remember her telling me about her a few times before.

But some guy is trying to hit on her.

I slip my feet in my shoes and slam the door behind me without thinking about what I'm doing. Right now, whether or not she wants to see me is irrelevant. Whether or not she does is even less relevant.

All I can think of in this second is getting down to Vibe and hauling this jackass off of my Dayton.

The music from the bar hits my ears as soon as I round the corner, and there are small pockets of people smoking outside. I push past them and into the bar.

My eyes immediately scan the place, searching for that gorgeous head of brown hair. She's not hard to find. I'm drawn to her like we're opposite poles. I'm certain I could find her even if the world was ending.

"Really, let me get it for you," some guy says, leaning into her.

"That's very kind of you, but no, thank you," she responds, her voice carrying over the music. She hands a bill to the guy working the bar and turns away from the one next to her.

I think he's about to speak again, but I don't know, because I interrupt him anyway. "You heard the lady. She can buy her own drink."

Dayton stiffens.

"And who are you?" he shoots back.

My lips tug up at one side. "I'm the owner."

"Right. Sure you are. I bet you just want her for yourself, don't you?"

I lean into him, lowering my voice. "I own this bar, and you'd be right in assuming that the woman you're attempting to hit on is mine also. Now I suggest you find a seat at the other end of the bar or I'll remove you personally."

He stares me down before grabbing his beer and moving. Dickhead.

Dayton grabs Liv's arm and they both stand. She tugs her toward the exit, and the second Dayton's hand falls from her friend, I step in. I shake my head at the blonde in front of me, and she shuts her mouth on whatever she was going to say.

The street is empty, the smokers of minutes ago back inside or moved on. The only person here is Dayton, leaning against the wall with her hands pressed against her stomach.

I step in front of her, my heart racing at the sight of her. Fuck. She looks gorgeous. Her dress clings to every part of her body, and her hair is parted to the side, hanging over one shoulder, tantalizingly showing the side of her neck. I want to bend forward and run my lips across her skin, fold her into me, slide my hands over her body.

And then she looks up, and I remember everything.

Her dark eyes are hard but shocked. "What the fuck are you doing here?"

"I own this place with my uncle. He saw you were here and called me."

"Not that it has anything to do with you. Where's Liv?" She straightens, ready to move, but I reach out.

My fingers wrap around her bicep and I spin her into me. This conversation isn't done yet.

"I wanted to see if you were okay. That's all. Then that guy—"

"I can take care of myself." She snatches her arm back. "I'm more than capable of it, thank you. I certainly don't need saving from someone who has no right to do so."

"Is that what you think?"

She steps back, her voice softening slightly. "That's what I know. You gave up every right to have anything to do with me eleven days ago."

"Twelve."

"What?"

A bitter laugh bubbles in my throat, but I swallow it down.

"Twelve days. But who's counting?"

"Not me, evidently." She turns away from me, leaving me with the view of the way her dress dips down to the small of her back, and rests her hand against the door.

"It's over." The words fall from me easily despite the desperation inside me. I need her to know this, know that the thing that broke us apart is done with. "Naomi finally signed the papers two days ago."

"Congratulations," she responds weakly. "Now perhaps you can find someone and have a real relationship with them."

I shake my head as I look at her, her profile illuminated by the flickering of the bar lights. "I already found her."

"Then it's a shame you fucked it up, isn't it?"

I step into her and rest my hand above hers on the door handle. My chest presses into her back, her ass perfectly curving against me, and I settle my hand on her waist. She needs to understand that I'm not letting her go.

I lower my mouth to her ear. "It took me seven years to find you again, and if you think I'm giving up now, you're so very, very wrong."

"I don't doubt that for a second, but it doesn't mean you'll get anywhere."

"This isn't over, Dayton. We aren't over."

"Oh, it is. We're very over. Trust me."

Like she's snapped out of a trance, she yanks on the door. The movement forces me to step back and let her back inside. I follow her in, allowing her to return to Liv, and watch her steadily. Her hips sway with each step, and something in my stomach twists when I see her reach up to the corner of her eye and smile wanly.

Then her eyes meet mine, a myriad of emotions swirling in them, all fighting for the limelight, for the consuming swamp of feeling. Heartbreak is the most prevalent, I notice, its shadows slightly darker than the regret and sadness that push against it.

I hope that, in my own, she sees the same thing reflected back.

The eyes speak louder than the mouth ever could.

The One Where He Waits At Her House

The thought of her working is haunting me the same way storm clouds hover threateningly. It's heavy and oppressing, ever-present.

In my heart, I don't believe she is. I don't believe for a second that she's sleeping with other men. It's in her eyes. I saw it in the way she looked at me outside the club. She can't possibly be giving her body to another man when it belongs so wholly to me. Only me.

Every inch of her, from the way her hair falls softly around her face to the way her toes curl when I look at her, belongs to me.

And the thought of her being with anyone else makes my skin crawl in a way I hope to never feel again. The anger that accompanies that sweeping sensation is tangible. It's dangerous, and if I were a lesser man, the feeling might frighten me. As it is, all it does is strengthen my resolve to win her back.

It merely strengthens my resolve to have her back where she belongs and have her stay there.

I still fail to understand what possesses her to be a call girl. I knew the only way I could protect her after she walked into the Southfall was by buying her, by having her off-limits to all other men. If I have to do the same again, I will.

I will do whatever it takes, pay whatever it costs, if it means I can keep her safe. Even if she never speaks to me again. She will never belong to anyone other than me. I am as certain of this as I am that I love her. My love for her and need to protect her are one and the same. There's no middle ground for it. There's no other option.

Just love her and protect her.

Whether she'll let me or not.

I pour a glass of water and look out the window. The sun is slowly beginning its descent toward the horizon, a hazy, golden glow emanating from it and mingling with the bright blue sky of the day. I gaze at the colors for a long while, watching as the bright circle lowers even farther.

The evening is when she works most. My skin crawls again, and I reach for the phone. "Hello, Jasper?"

"Yes, Mr. Stone. What can I do for you, sir?"

"Have my car brought around for me, would you?"

"Absolutely. It'll be waiting for you when you get downstairs."

"Thank you." I put the phone back in the holder and grab my jacket from the hooks. I slip my arms into it and step into the elevator, my mind running a thousand miles an hour.

I use these minutes in the elevator to justify my decisions. To justify going to her house. But fucking hell. I need to know if she's there or not. If she's not, there's a good chance she's working. And if that's the case, I won't be leaving so fucking quietly.

Like Jasper said, the car is waiting for me, and I slip in with ease. I give the driver Dayton's address and lean back, closing my eyes.

I hope she's not working. My fists clench at the thought of another man's hands touching her body. The image forms in my mind before I can banish it, and it taunts me. All I can see is her lying back on a bed and fingertips trailing across her silky skin… Dipping inside her hip and across her mound…

I open my eyes and realize that isn't an imagined situation. It's real, a memory. A memory of my own hands skimming across her body and touching her in the most intimate way.

That is almost worse. The memory of her with me is almost worse than the thought of her with another.

That's how much it hurts to miss her.

The car slows as we approach her house, and I look out the window. Her house is in darkness. Every light is off. The curtains are open, but I can only make out the outline of furniture in the waning light.

"Stop the car," I order, unbuckling my seatbelt. It slams into the seat with the same vigor I open my car door with. "Drive around the block and park down the street. Wait there for me."

"Yes, sir."

The car door slams with an almost-satisfying clunk. I turn to her house—her empty house.

She's working.

I know it.

I storm up the pathway leading to her front door and knock on it several times. When there's no answer, I call her name. After a couple of minutes of fruitless attempts, I hear a voice from the next yard.

"She went out earlier," an elderly woman informs me.

"Thank you. I'll wait here for her." I smile at her kindly despite the myriad of emotions swirling in my stomach.

She returns the smile. "Dressed up real pretty, she was. Always looks beautiful. Quiet girl though. Keeps to herself."

"That sounds like Dayton. Thank you, ma'am. I'm sorry if I disturbed you."

"No, no, you didn't. Would you like some tea while you wait?"

"I'm fine. Thank you."

She nods and shuts the window. I run my fingers through my hair and sit on the bench in Dayton's yard. My elbows rest on top of my knees, and I bury my face in my hands for a long moment.

Fuck. I can't believe she's working. I can't believe she can look at me with heartbreak in her eyes and then be with another fucking man!

I dig the heels of my hands in my eyes. I'm completely damn lost. If I had any idea where she was tonight, I'd march down there and drag her away. Fuck appearances. If I had any idea where she was, she'd be leaving with me.

After what seems like hours but is probably mere minutes, I hear the angry slam of a car door and look up.

My first thought is how fucking beautiful she looks storming toward me with her hair flying over her shoulders. The next is that she's alone.

"If this happens again, Mr. Stone, I may have to look into taking legal action. Two nights in a row? I hardly imagine your sitting outside my house is a coincidence."

I find her eyes with mine. Her anger is so evident it shines like a beacon, so strong I can almost feel it reaching out and wrapping around my body.

"Back to work, Miss Black?"

"I have a job. As much as I'd love to sit around and feel sorry for myself, I'm afraid I have far more important things to do." She tears her eyes from mine and steps toward her front door, digging her key from her purse.

Running, again. She's always fucking running.

I stand and grab her hand. "Things, or people?"

"I fail to see what business it is of yours." Her sharp tone cuts through me, but I fight through the annoyance to keep my calm.

"It's very much my business, as you're well aware."

"Perhaps in your opinion. But if it will make you feel better, it's things, not people." She turns, and the sick feeling in my stomach dissipates. "I'm not back to work fully. Yet."

I tighten my grip on her hand. My jaw clenches, and it takes everything I have to bite out the word. "Yet?"

"I have to earn money somehow, and my big spenders aren't pretty little rich boys who need a date for the night. So yes, yet."

Her defiance riles me. It raises every hair on the back of my neck and stokes every primal, protective instinct inside my body.

I lean into her. "Never. You aren't fucking another guy, Dayton."

"That's not your decision, Aaron. You had your chance to decide that, and you blew it. Now if you'd like to remove yourself from my property, I'd appreciate it."

Not a fucking chance, I think before lowering my lips to hers. I take her mouth forcefully, covering her red lips with my own. The pressure of my body against hers pushes her flat against her door, and I lean into her, aware of the hardening of my cock. The tiny whimper that escapes her tells me that she's aware of it too, and her body responds the way it always does.

Her hips grind into mine, and I cup her face with my hands. I hold her still, reminding her who has the control here, and push my tongue between her lips. She tastes sweet and fruity, almost as if she's had a drink or two tonight.

"Tell me one thing," I demand, my voice rough and low. "Has anyone else kissed these lips?" I tug on her bottom one with my thumb.

"Fuck you," she whispers, her voice wavering.

"Answer the fucking question, Dayton."

"No. They haven't."

I curl one hand around the back of her neck and close the distance between us yet again. This time, I'm even harsher. An unnecessary reminder of who she is to me. What she is to me.

That no one else will ever kiss her the way I am now.

My tongue sweeps through her mouth, and she melts beneath me. Her fingers clench at my shirt, holding me tight to her, and I want to rip that fucking key out of her hand. I want to shove her through this door, lay her flat on her bed, and fuck her until she gets the message I'm so desperately trying to convey with my mouth.

I want to fuck her until she understands that this won't be the last time I kiss her.

I pull back, grazing her bottom lip with my teeth the way I know she likes, and rest my nose alongside hers. Both of our chests are rising and falling quickly, and I'd bet everything I have that her heart is thumping the way mine is.

Dayton takes a long, shuddery breath and drops her hands from my shirt. Her eyes are full of fire when they find mine. "You have five seconds to get your ass out of here before I go crazy at you."

I smirk, reveling in that anger. It means she got the message.

"Remember that the next time you think what you do is none of my business." I brush my thumb across her mouth one last time. Our gazes lock as I walk backward down her pathway and wave my hand. The car pulls up behind me and I open the door. "Good evening, Dayton."

She simply stares at me as I get into the vehicle. Just before I close my door, I hear her front door slam.

"Back to the apartment," I order the driver.

HIS CALL

He pulls away silently. I pull my cell from my pocket with shaky hands and dial Monique's number.

She's not getting away that easily.

The One Where Her Secret Comes Out

I rub my temples harshly. This contract negotiation is such a fucking headache. If it weren't the one that could push us over the billion-dollar mark, I'd hand it off to someone else. I'd let my employees do what I damn well pay them for.

"Five years is unreasonable. We're offering one campaign, not several."

"And we're offering you more. I fail to understand why this is an issue in our negotiations."

"I'd like to see the outcome of one campaign before hiring your services again."

"Are you doubting our ability, sir?"

"Enough!" I raise my voice over the endless back and forth. The room immediately silences, and I turn my attention to the gentleman sitting opposite me. "Mr. Simmons, with all due respect, you're asking us to put all our manpower behind this latest line. No one here is doubting the inevitable success your wife is about to have. Her designs are truly remarkable, and the interest she has already garnered for her next collection is impressive. This will absolutely cement her place in the fashion world, but from a business perspective, I cannot take just one campaign of this caliber."

He opens his mouth to respond, but I continue.

"You are essentially asking me to turn away a selection of smaller contracts because of the scale of your own. I refuse to do this, but I'm willing to take on staff to accommodate for your needs. In turn, this will take time to hire them. Do you understand it from my perspective? If I'm going to do this, I need more than one campaign for you."

"Five years is incredibly long, Mr. Stone. That's ten collections of my wife's."

The door opens and Dottie pokes her head in. "Excuse me. Mr. Stone, there's an important call for you."

"Can't it wait?"

Her eyes widen in a message I don't understand and she shakes her head.

I sigh. "Excuse me, everyone. Let's take ten minutes and come back to this. Dottie, can you have some coffee sent up?"

She nods, and I follow her from the room.

Loosening my tie, I pick up the phone in my office. "Aaron

Stone."

"Aaron." Tyler's voice is slightly panicked. "You need to come home. Dayton's freaking out."

I frown. "Freaking out?"

"She's having a panic attack. I can't calm her down."

I drop the phone without responding and exit my office quicker than I entered it. "Dottie, clear my afternoon. We'll continue this meeting in the morning. Nine a.m. sharp. I want every detail spread out before then."

"Of course. Is everything okay?"

"It will be."

I ride down the building in the elevator and climb into my waiting car. Panic attack? Dayton? She's the most composed woman I know. I can't imagine anything that would have her upset to such an extreme.

Worry floods my body. Something truly terrible must have happened. But what?

My mind conjures up any number of situations, all completely ridiculous, and it's only silenced by the sound of the engine cutting outside my apartment block.

I jog across the lobby and into the elevator, jabbing at the buttons the whole way. Of course, it's completely ridiculous. It won't make it go any faster, and although it's only been a matter of seconds, it feels like an hour.

I burst through the apartment door and see Tyler kneeling in front of Dayton in the middle of the kitchen. Her labored breaths fill the air and pained whimpers cut through me. I push Ty out of the way and frame her face with my hands.

"Dayton. Breathe for me, sweetheart. Come on now. Breathe."

She shudders beneath my touch and takes a long, controlled breath.

"That's it. And out. And back in. That's better." I fold her into my arms.

Her cheek is flat against my chest, and I gently rock her side to side until she calms. She's shaking against me, and she feels so tiny in my arms.

And I know something is very, very wrong.

"I'm glad you were here," I say to Tyler, barely glancing over my shoulder at him.

"Sorry I pulled you from your meeting, cuz."

"Fuck the meeting. The contract will still be there tomorrow morning." I tilt Dayton's face up so she's looking at me. "What's wrong?"

Fear and guilt fill her eyes. My body tenses in response to it, especially when her bottom lip quivers.

"I have to tell you something," she whispers.

Something I won't like. "What is it? What's wrong?"

She flicks her eyes over my shoulder to Tyler and her breath catches. "Naomi came to see me just before we went to London."

My arms fall away from her. Shock is smacking me in the gut.

Naomi? What the fuck is going on? "What?"

Dayton pulls herself to a standing position and leans on the bar. Her hands are still shaking. "She wasn't happy with the divorce settlement, and she came to ask me for money."

Tyler snorts. I look at him then back to Dayton. He knew.

"You knew about this?" I question him.

My cousin nods.

I swallow down the rapidly rising anger in my body and turn back to Dayton. "She asked you for money? Why didn't you just tell me?"

"She didn't…ask…so much as blackmail me."

"How much?"

"Two and a half million."

Two and a half fucking million dollars? "What the fucking hell, Dayton!"

"She gave me four weeks to get it to her, and I have one week left."

I close my eyes briefly, breathing in, and wait for her to continue.

"When I went home after London, there was a letter waiting, and today, there was one delivered here. She's keeping tabs on me. She knows Tyler knows and she said if I told you all bets were off."

"All bets for what? What could she possibly know about you that she could hold over your head?"

She gives me a piece of paper, her head down. "She knows I was a call girl. If I don't pay, she's threatening to expose my past and destroy your business."

I look down at the white sheet in my hand and the words written there.

One week. Doesn't time fly when you're having fun? It's a shame you told Tyler... I'll let it pass. You're getting desperate, after all. But if you tell Aaron...the world will meet Mia Lopez.

My chest tightens in anger. No, this is more than anger. This is pure fucking fury.

I knew Naomi was a manipulative bitch, but I never imagined that she would go this far. To drag Dayton into our bullshit is uncalled for and completely unnecessary.

And the fact she never told me…

I look up. She can't even look at me. I know how she feels. I felt the same way in Paris.

Slowly, she looks up, and her broken brown eyes meet mine. She shrinks back, wrapping her arms around her stomach. I crumple the paper to the floor and turn away. I need to get out of here, get away from her. I need to escape from the knowledge that another secret is coming between us and my vile ex-wife is the center of it yet again.

The door slams behind me with a certain finality. It's a deafening sound that echoes down the stairwell. The elevator is no good for this...this anger. There's no outlet.

But not even the harsh pounding of my feet against the stairs can beat this anger out.

I pull out my cell and call the office. Dottie answers almost immediately.

"Find out where Naomi is living. Now."

My cell is snatched from my hand, and I turn to see Tyler bringing it to his ear. "Ignore that, Dottie. He's having a bad day." My cousin pockets the phone and looks at me.

"What the fuck, Ty?"

He grabs my arm and leads me through the lobby. "Going over there when you're this angry isn't going to solve anything. What you need, mate, is a drink."

I don't want a drink. I want to find out why the woman I love kept such a huge fucking secret from me. Why she's been dealing with this shit alone when I could have dealt with it weeks ago.

Still, I allow Tyler to lead me to the nearest bar and order two glasses of whisky. I drain mine in one go and nod to the bartender for another. The liquid burns as it goes down, taking away from the anger settling in my chest.

"When did she tell you?" I ask Tyler, staring straight ahead.

"In London. After she came to Jenna's shoot," he replies. "She froze every time Naomi's name was mentioned and I wanted to know why."

"You pushed her into telling you?"

"Pushed her into telling you, too. She was going to tonight. The letter threw everything off course."

I swallow, my throat dry despite my constant sipping. I feel utter disbelief. Dayton made it very clear in Paris how much she despises secrets. She berated me endlessly for having kept Naomi from her, and now, in a cruel twist of irony, she's done the exact same thing.

For the last three weeks, she's been carrying this around. Through everything we've dealt with, she's kept this fucking secret.

She stood in front of me and asked me to bear my soul to her when she wasn't doing the same thing. She wanted me to be open when she was unable to do it herself.

"Why didn't she tell me?" I face Tyler now.

He shrugs a shoulder with a heavy sigh. "She wanted to protect you. She didn't want you to worry about it. She felt like it was her problem, not yours."

I rub my hands across my face. It hurts more than it angers me. The fact that Naomi could do this, could blackmail Dayton for her own selfish needs, angers me beyond belief. I feel that fury grasping on to my body, but the hurt from Dayton not being able to tell me overcomes it.

I slump onto the bar, fisting my hair. Suddenly, all too acutely, I feel the pain she must have felt in Paris.

"Fuck," I breathe heavily. "I can't believe she's been coping with this by herself."

"She's determined, that's for sure. I offered to help her out and she pretty much fucking laughed at me. I've never known anyone so independent, if you discount Tessa." Tyler chuckles.

It's easy to imagine—Dayton laughing at him. She doesn't take being helped well.

I drink the rest of my drink and stand up. "Come with me."

Tyler follows me from the bar. "What are you doing?"

I know that the store is down this street. It's a personal favorite of my mother, one my dad has visited time and time again. Right now, I'm thanking him for having shown me it.

"Mate, you're fucking mental," Tyler explodes when we stop in the front of the jewelers.

A small laugh leaves me. "No, I'm just a presumptuous bastard."

"What the hell are you thinking?"

I look at my cousin. "I'm thinking Naomi already came between us once and I'm not letting it happen again. I'm also thinking Day will kill me when I ask her, but it's about the only thing that will calm me now. I need to know that, one day, the ring I'm about to purchase will be on that woman's finger before I can go ahead and deal with the one who never should have had a ring in the first place."

***

She looks so peaceful lying in our bed, tangled in the sheets. She's curled into a tiny ball, illuminated only by the light shining in through the gap in the curtains. But still, she's so beautiful. So fucking beautiful.

I strip silently, leaving my clothes in a heap on the floor before climbing into bed next to her. She curls up tighter, and I know she's not asleep, so I reach forward and pull her into my arms.

She sighs heavily as I tangle our bodies together and bury my face in her neck. Her hair tickles my nose, and the gentle scent of vanilla grounds me.

"What are you doing?" she whispers. I can hear the tears in her voice and it breaks my heart.

I kiss her shoulder and squeeze her to me. "I'm holding you, baby. What else do you think I'm doing?"

"You shouldn't be. You should hate me."

I shake my head, pulling her onto her back. Leaning over her, I gaze down into her sad eyes. Silly, silly woman.

"I could never hate you, Dayton. Not ever." A tear escapes the corner of her eye and I brush it away with my thumb, leaving my hand lying beside her face. "So don't say such ridiculous things."

She cups my cheek. "Why aren't you mad at me?"

"Because you didn't keep it a secret to spite me. You kept it to protect me, and yes, it was a little misguided and unnecessary, but you did it because you care."

"But you did that, too, and I left you."

I close the distance between our mouths and kiss her with the same certainty I purchased two rings with earlier. "I'm not leaving you, beautiful woman, so get that thought right out of your pretty little head. I'm not going anywhere and neither are you."

"But you did. Earlier. When you found out. You left then."

There's so much fear in her eyes. *Oh, sweetheart.*

"Because I was a kind of angry I never want you to see," I say softly. "But it wasn't at you. Not entirely, anyway. Most of it was at her, and if you hadn't sent Tyler after me, I just might have found her apartment and done something incredibly stupid."

"I'm sorry." She hugs me tightly, and I roll us onto our sides. I tuck her into my body, holding her so tight that I'm afraid I may snap her.

I know how sorry she is. It's in every unsaid word and every unshed tear.

"I know. We'll talk some more in the morning, okay? Get some sleep now."

"Never go to sleep on an argument," she mutters. "That's what my mom always taught me. You sort it out first."

"Bambi, we're not arguing. Not even close." I gently sweep my thumb over her eyelids, making her close her eyes, and rest one of her arms over my waist. She flattens her hand against my back, splaying her fingers. "Now we're going to go to sleep together and wake up the same way, today and every day. Understand?"

She buries her face into my neck with a nod. "I don't deserve you."

That thought is so absurd, and I almost laugh as I kiss her head. "And I don't deserve you, so I guess we're even. Goodnight, sweetheart."

The One With The Red Outfit

I shut the door behind me and leave the keys on the table next to me. The house is completely silent—bar Dayton singing quietly upstairs. My lips curve into a gentle smile, and I pause at the bottom of the stairs, just listening to her slightly out-of-tune voice ramble the words of some song.

I can barely believe she's mine, this unbelievably gorgeous woman. After everything we've been through, sometimes I have to touch her to make sure she's real and not a figment of my imagination. That this time, we're getting it right, with no secrets or lies.

This is nothing but me and the woman I have loved for as long as I remember in our Parisian hideaway.

I quietly walk upstairs, my eyes on the cracked-open bedroom door the whole time. Her voice fades into a low hum in another tune I don't recognize. I flatten my hand against the door and push silently, stepping into the room.

My gaze tumbles over her body. She's lying on her front in the middle of the bed with her dark hair falling over her shoulders, her knees bent and swinging back and forth behind her.

But that's not what is holding my attention. That would be the red lace molded to her body and the round curve of her bare ass. The black stockings with a red seam running up the back of her legs. My dick hardens at the sight of her and she hasn't even registered my presence yet. I take advantage of this and the fact she's facing away from me as I slip off my shoes.

I cross the room on tiptoes and jump onto the bed over her. Dayton screams and attempts to roll over, but I grab her wrists and hold her down where she is.

"Well, hello there." I drop a kiss to her bare shoulder, and she relaxes.

"Aaron, you bastard. You scared the shit out of me." She flicks her legs up and nudges me in the back with curled toes.

I smile against her skin. "I'm sorry. My first instinct was to jump on you when I saw you."

She turns her head to the side, and I lean back so she can meet my eyes. "Oh, you like this, then?" She wriggles, her ass rubbing against my cock doing nothing for the throbbing erection I possess. "It's just something I threw on."

"Like it? I was wondering when you were going to wear this for me." I release her wrists and let her roll over.

She looks up at me with dark eyes full of seduction and runs her hands up my arms. "I wasn't going to make you wait too long. It was expensive, after all."

My eyes flit to the way the outfit pushes her gorgeous tits together, and I palm one gently. "It was worth every penny," I murmur, dropping my face to hers.

She takes my sweeping kiss, and her tongue meets mine thrust for thrust. Her fingers tangle in my hair, and I groan, firmly squeezing her breast.

"Were you planning to seduce me, Miss Black?"

She gasps when I run my lips down her neck and nip lightly. "Whatever gives you that idea, Mr. Stone?"

A primal thrill runs through me like it always does when she says my name.

"The red lace… The string panties… The stockings… You're just missing a pair of red heels."

"It can be arranged."

I get off of her and pull her into a sitting position. "Not can be. It has been. Get your ass off this bed and put those heels on, Dayton. And this is not a demand."

She sighs, swinging her legs over the side of the bed, and shoots a flirty glance over her shoulder as she saunters to the closet. "Gosh, I love your requirements."

My lips curve into a smirk, and I watch her put the shoes on. "And I love how you're always so willing to fulfill them."

Dayton walks to me, temptation embodied, and her own lips,

which are coated in red, mirror mine. "Always, as long as you never ask me nicely."

Her hands rest on my shoulders, and I grasp her waist. I tug her harshly to me so that she falls to her knees on the bed. Given that her ass is touching her heels and I'm kneeling up, her head is tilted back slightly so she can look up at me.

I love seeing her on her knees. There's only one thing wrong with this—and if she doesn't want to be asked nicely, I'm happy to oblige. More than fucking happy to.

I bend my face to hers and kiss her harshly. "Get off this bed and go to the window."

She does as I say without another word. Without her usual sass or snark. I follow her to the large bay window and unbuckle my pants. Her tongue flicks across her lips, her eyes following the movement of my fingers, and I grow even harder.

I slide my boxer briefs and pants down in one swift movement and sit on the seat beneath the window. I motion for her to come over, and when she's standing in front of me, I reach up and wrap my hand around the back of her neck. She bends forward, bringing her face to mine, her breathing erratic.

"Get on your knees."

I ease her down, my hand still curved around her neck, and she looks at me expectantly. She knows what I'm going to say—that is evident by the naughty yet wanting spark in her eyes—but she wants to hear the words.

She loves words. I've noticed that. If I tried hard enough, I could probably bring her to orgasm with them alone.

"Now," I say slowly, grasping her wrist and bringing her hand to my dick. "Wrap those pretty little lips around my cock and suck me until your throat is raw."

Her lips quirk before she wraps her fingers around me and opens her mouth. I close my eyes at the first flick of her tongue across my head. She closes her lips around me and draws me into her mouth in one long suck.

She works me easily yet intensely, her hand twisting in time with the bobbing of her head as she takes me ever deeper into her throat. My hand makes its way into her hair and fists the silky locks. My other hand stays firmly clenched around the edge of the seat, letting her keep to her own rhythm and pace.

And fuck. This woman can tease my cock into rock. She runs her tongue up the length of my shaft and looks up. I meet her eyes and groan loudly. Her red lips around my dick truly is my favorite sight.

When I feel as if I can take no more of the sweet heat of her mouth around me, I pull her head back and her to a standing position.

For the first time since seeing it, I berate this outfit. The coverage of it means there's a small strip of skin above the tiny panty line stretching over her hips, and I have to dip my head to kiss her there. I palm her tight ass with one hand to hold her to me and massage one of her tits with the other. My lips brush over her exposed skin, and I hear her sigh.

"Wet, baby?" I ask against her. My fingers creep over her ass and slip between her legs. It answers my question. Yes, she's wet. She has fucking soaked this excuse for a pair of panties. "These are coming off."

I tug them down her legs and she steps out of them. She rakes her fingers through her hair, and I look up at her, dipping the tip of my finger inside her pussy. Her legs twitch as she opens them slightly, and I stand.

We spin at my insistence, and I bring her hands to the buttons on my shirt. She undoes them one by one and slides the light material down my arms.

I brush my thumb across her cheek, down her neck, across the curve of her tits… "Get on your knees."

"Again?" she quips.

"Smartass." I grab her shoulders, turn her so she's facing the window, and bring my mouth to her ear. "Get on your knees and rest your elbows on that seat."

Her chest hitches just before she moves. But she does.

"Open your legs."

Her ass jerks as she slides her knees across the carpet. "Like this?" she asks almost breathlessly.

I kneel behind her and spread her ass cheeks with my hands, my eyes falling on her glistening cunt. "Yes. Just like that, baby."

I flick my tongue against her folds without a warning. She tastes so fucking sweet. A long, low moan escapes her lips when I lick a slow path from her asshole to her clit, putting pressure on that swollen, tender bundle of nerves.

"Like that?" I ask against her.

"Mhmm," she moans back, arching her back so her ass tilts up and I have even easier access to her pussy.

I lick her harder, delighting in every whimper and moan that comes from her mouth and every writhe and wriggle of her hips. I circle her clit firmly, and when her cries escalate, signaling her impending orgasm, I stop.

"What—"

I push my cock inside her before she can finish her sentence, and she throws her head back. She mumbles something unintelligible.

"How long were you wearing this before I returned?" I question, holding myself deep inside her. "Answer, Dayton."

"I changed when you left."

"So two hours?"

"Yes," she breathes.

I slowly ease out of her and slide my hand up her back to her hair. Soft. Silky. Perfect for wrapping my fingers in and tugging on.

Her head arches back when I do just that.

"Two hours in this sexy-as-fuck outfit and you didn't tell me." I tsk, continuing my slow, easy thrusts into her. "I should carry on fucking you like this to punish you for that."

"Punish me? Oh!"

"Yes. For wearing this and not telling me. I know you hate it slow. You like it hard and fast, don't you, baby?"

She clenches her hands into fists. "No. Hate it hard."

I flatten my hand against her stomach and lean against her back. I nip her shoulder with my teeth. "You're a dirty liar, Ms. Black."

"Would you like me to beg for it hard and fast, Mr. Stone? Would that make up for not telling you about this little red number?"

"No. Convince me you hate it hard and I might just be persuaded." I twist her head to the side and pull out of her, leaving only the head of my cock buried inside her hot, wet pussy.

"Worst thing ever. Not great at all. I much prefer it slow. Mhmm."

I thrust into her quickly and I'm rewarded by a high-pitched squeak from her lips. "Oh, yes. I can hear how much you despise it when I fuck you hard."

"You're playing with me, Aaron."

"I enjoy playing with you very much." I circle her clit with my thumb. "And you enjoy it also."

"You know, you can fuck without talking."

I remove my hand, grasp her hips before digging my fingers in, and pick up the pace. Her pussy walls clench around my cock, making her even tighter, and the slight gyrate to her hips meets my thrusts. But no sounds leave her lips, no whimpers, no moans, no sighs.

"We can fuck without talking—you're correct—but you much prefer it when I whisper dirty things in your ear, don't you, Dayton?" I lean back so I can enter her farther. "You much prefer it when I tell you I love the way your cunt tightens around me, how wet you get, how easily my cock slips inside you. You much prefer hearing how gorgeous your ass looks bouncing in front of me as I fuck you hard." My palm connects with her ass, and she moans. "Don't you?"

"Yes," she whimpers. "I do."

Good. I much prefer telling her how fucking hard she gets me, how hard I want to fuck her, how fucking gorgeous she looks bent over before me.

So I do. I lean forward, resting my hands next to hers on the seat, and whisper all those things in her ear. Until her cries reach a crescendo and her pussy clenches hard, pulling my own release from me.

I spill into her in short, hot spurts, and her name repeatedly tumbles from my lips. My body is shaking with the intensity of our release, and I link my fingers through hers. I sit up, pulling her back with me, and wrap our arms around her stomach.

Dayton drops her head back onto my shoulder, and I turn my face into her. She shivers when my lips brush her neck and reaches back to cup the back of my head.

"Wow," she breathes, laughter creeping through into her voice. "If I knew that would happen, I would have worn that outfit weeks ago."

I laugh quietly. "Oh, baby, that's one outfit you can wear whenever you want. In fact, I'll be offended if you aren't wearing it when I get home every day."

She laughs loudly and shakes my arms off. She climbs off me and turns, grinning, laying her hands on my shoulders. "I'm not here to be your sex slave, Mr. Stone. Whether you require it or not."

I grab her wrist and pull her down, falling backward onto the floor. Her laughter is magical as she falls with me, and my lips curl into a happy smile. Being like this with her, so happy and free, gives me a light feeling I haven't felt in a long time.

"Really? You're not? I thought that was the agreement!"

She slaps my chest. "You pig. You are supposed to love me and cherish me."

I raise an eyebrow, sensing that there's more.

"And fuck me whenever you can."

"That comes under the loving and cherishing. It's a given, baby. And since I plan to love you and cherish you every single day…" I trail off, grinning up at her, and let her fill in the blanks.

She smiles, amusement dancing in her gorgeous eyes as she gets up. "You little word-twister, you."

I laugh. "I'm a man. I'll always turn things to my favor, especially sexually."

I stand, grab her wrists, and throw her onto the bed. She shrieks, and I drop myself over her. She tilts her head to the side, gazing up at me.

I lower my mouth to hers and nip her bottom lip. "Now, should we get back to that loving and cherishing thing?"

About the Author

By day, *New York Times* and *USA Today* bestselling New Adult author Emma Hart dons a cape and calls herself Super Mum to two beautiful little monsters. By night, she drops the cape, pours a glass of whatever she fancies – usually wine – and writes books.

Emma is working on Top Secret projects she will share with her followers and fans at every available opportunity. Naturally, all Top Secret projects involve a dashingly hot guy who likes to forget to wear a shirt, a sprinkling (or several) of hold-onto-your-panties hot scenes, and a whole lotta love.

She likes to be busy - unless busy involves doing the dishes, but that seems to be when all the ideas come to life.

Find Emma online at:

Blog: http://www.emmahart.org

Facebook: www.facebook.com/EmmaHartBooks

Twitter: @EmmaHartAuthor

Goodreads: http://www.goodreads.com/author/show/6451162.Emma_Hart

Printed in Great Britain
by Amazon.co.uk, Ltd.,
Marston Gate.